This edition published by Parragon Books Ltd in 2015

Parragon Books Ltd
Chartist House
15–17 Trim Street
Bath BA1 1HA, UK
www.parragon.com

ISBN 978-1-4723-9100-1

Printed in China

FROM THE MOVIE

Disney · PIXAR

INSIDE
OUT

PaRragon

Bath • New York • Cologne • Melbourne • Delhi
Hong Kong • Shenzhen • Singapore • Amsterdam

When a little girl called Riley was born, her first Emotion, Joy, ran Headquarters from inside Riley's mind. As Joy watched what happened to Riley on a big screen, memory spheres were created.

Joy picked up the first memory – it showed Riley as a baby. It was gold because the sphere contained a happy memory. Joy placed the sphere on a shelf in Headquarters.

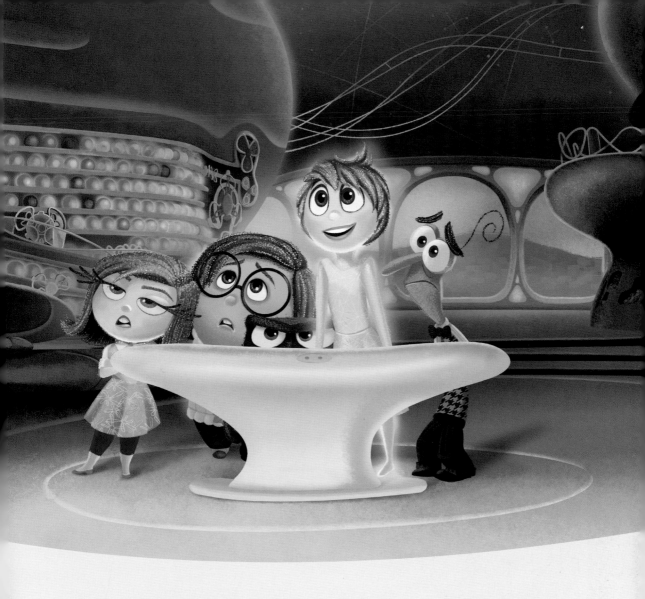

As Riley grew older, the shelves in Headquarters became full of memory spheres. Joy was also joined by four more Emotions – Sadness, Disgust, Anger and Fear.

Together, the Five Emotions made important choices for Riley from the console inside her mind. Joy was the leader and all she wanted was for the little girl to be happy.

Fear helped keep Riley safe.
He once stopped her from tripping
over a power cable when she was
running through the house.

Disgust kept Riley away
from things that looked,
smelled or tasted funny.
Like broccoli!

Anger cared very deeply about
things being fair. All of Riley's
tantrums happened when Anger was
driving the console.

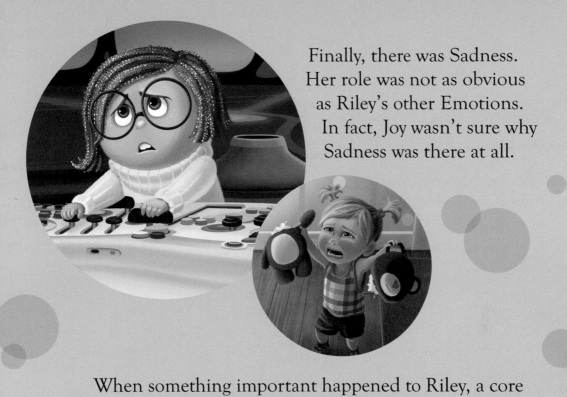

Finally, there was Sadness. Her role was not as obvious as Riley's other Emotions. In fact, Joy wasn't sure why Sadness was there at all.

When something important happened to Riley, a core memory was created. Each core memory powered Riley's Islands of Personality.

There were five islands – Goofball, Friendship, Hockey, Honesty and Family.

When Riley was 11, her mum and dad announced that they were moving from their home town in Minnesota, to San Francisco. The Emotions panicked! Riley had great friends and a lovely home in Minnesota. Things couldn't have been better there.

After a long car journey, Riley and her parents arrived at their new house in San Francisco. Riley was miserable that she had to move, but Joy desperately tried to keep Riley happy by taking control of the console.

Before long, it was Riley's first day at her new school. Joy gave each Emotion an important job to do.

Joy was determined to keep Riley happy on her first day at school. She carefully drew a circle of chalk on the floor round Sadness.

"This is the circle of sadness – your job today is to make sure that all of the sadness stays inside," she told Sadness.

At school Riley was asked to tell the class something about herself. Riley shared a happy memory of playing hockey back in Minnesota. But suddenly her smile faded and she became upset.

Joy saw that Sadness had left her circle and touched the hockey memory sphere, turning it blue! As Riley cried in front of her class, her first blue core memory was created.

In an attempt to get rid of the new sad core memory, Joy turned on the memory vacuum. Sadness tried to take the memory from Joy but in the chaos Joy, Sadness and all six core memories were sucked up the memory vacuum tube.

Joy and Sadness were sucked out of Headquarters and dumped out in Long Term Memory. All the Islands of Personality had turned dark, since the core memories weren't in the holder to power them up. Joy knew they had to get the memories back to Headquarters so the Islands would work again.

But Headquarters was far away. Joy collected up the five yellow core memories and both she and Sadness headed across a bridge to Goofball Island.

"But what if we fall into the Memory Dump?" asked Sadness. "We'd be forgotten about forever!"

"We won't fall," Joy answered. "Just think positive."

Joy had just made it to Goofball Island when it began to crumble. It was collapsing because Riley had got angry with her parents and stopped goofing around with her dad.

Joy grabbed Sadness and made it back to Long Term Memory just before the island disappeared into the dump. Sadness looked back at where the island had stood and realized that they could lose the other Islands of Personality, too.

Joy tried to stay positive – they would just have to make their way to another island, through the winding shelves of Long Term Memory.

But Sadness slumped to the floor in a puddle of despair as she thought about the islands collapsing. So Joy picked up one of her legs and dragged her along.

Back in Riley's bedroom, Riley was chatting to her old friend Meg on her laptop.

Meg told Riley about a new girl on the hockey team. Riley missed playing hockey with her old friends so the news made her angry.

At Headquarters, Anger took charge of the console and flames roared out of the top of his head.

Back in Long Term Memory, Joy and Sadness heard a loud groan as Friendship Island fell into the dump.

Joy looked up to Hockey Island. "We'll just have to go the long way round," she said, trying hard to stay positive.

As Joy and Sadness tried to find their way to Hockey Island they bumped into a funny-looking creature.

"You're Bing Bong!" Joy said excitedly. "You were Riley's imaginary friend!"

Riley and Bing Bong used to play together – they even had a rocket wagon that was powered by a song. But over the years, Riley had forgotten him.

Bing Bong told Joy that he was in Long Term Memory looking for a good memory so that Riley could remember him and he could be part of her life again.

"You know what? We're on our way to Headquarters. Come with us and we'll get Riley to remember you!" said Joy.

Bing Bong gave Joy his bag to carry the core memories in and told them that it would be much quicker to catch the Train of Thought to Headquarters.

"There's a station in Imagination Land," he said. "Come on, this way!"

The three of them reached Imagination Land just as the train pulled away, but Bing Bong knew how to get to another station through Imagination Land.

Once inside, Joy and Sadness were amazed! There was a French Fry Forest, Trophy Town and Cloud Town.

They soon reached a House of Cards, where Bing Bong found his rocket wagon. They also found the Imaginary Boyfriend Generator.

Meanwhile, Riley was at the try-outs for a new hockey team.

At Headquarters, Anger, Disgust and Fear tried to get Riley through it. But the Emotions couldn't find the right memory to replace the missing core memory. Riley missed the puck, fell over and then stormed off.

Inside Riley's mind Hockey Island fell to pieces and sank into the Memory Dump.

Joy, Sadness and Bing Bong watched in horror from the gates of Preschool World.

Inside Preschool World, some Mind Workers took Bing Bong's rocket wagon and threw it into the Memory Dump.

"No!" yelled Bing Bong. He sat on the floor and cried sweets. Joy tried to cheer him up, but nothing worked.

Sadness sat beside Bing Bong. "I'm sorry they took your rocket wagon," she said.

After they talked about how he felt, he said, "I feel okay now."

Joy was surprised. Sadness hadn't made Bing Bong feel worse, she had made him feel better!

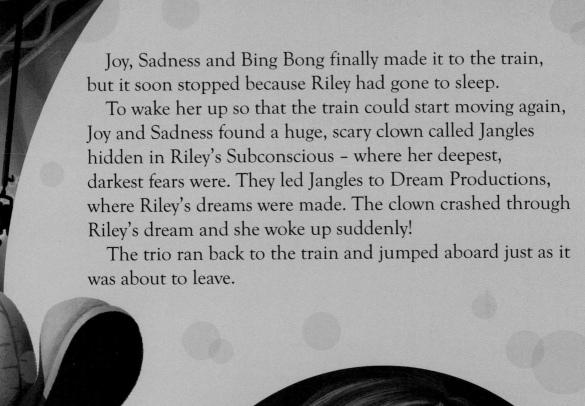

Joy, Sadness and Bing Bong finally made it to the train, but it soon stopped because Riley had gone to sleep.

To wake her up so that the train could start moving again, Joy and Sadness found a huge, scary clown called Jangles hidden in Riley's Subconscious – where her deepest, darkest fears were. They led Jangles to Dream Productions, where Riley's dreams were made. The clown crashed through Riley's dream and she woke up suddenly!

The trio ran back to the train and jumped aboard just as it was about to leave.

Meanwhile, at Headquarters, Anger had plugged an idea bulb into the console. After everything that had happened, and without Joy around to help, Anger decided that the best thing for Riley was to run away – back to Minnesota.

After the bulb was plugged into the console, the idea popped into Riley's head just as she woke up from her scary dream.

Riley needed money to buy a bus ticket to Minnesota so she sneaked downstairs and took money from her mum's purse.

Back on the Train of Thought, Joy heard a loud noise and looked out of the train carriage to see Honesty Island fall into the deep dump.

Suddenly the tracks underneath the train crumbled away and the train crashed into the cliffside. Everyone on the train jumped off just before it tipped over the cliff edge into the dump below.

"That was our way home!" Joy cried. "We lost another island.... What is happening?"

"Haven't you heard?" replied a worker from the train. "Riley is running away."

After the train crash, Sadness realized they could use a recall tube in Long Term Memory to get back to Headquarters. But as Joy got sucked up the tube, the cliff underneath them began to break apart. The tube broke and Joy fell deep into the Memory Dump!

At that moment, Riley was heading to the bus station, feeling nothing.

Down in the dump, Joy felt hopeless. She looked at a memory of a time when Riley had been sad but her friends had come to cheer her up. Suddenly Joy realized that Sadness was important – Riley's friends came to help because she was sad!

Just then, Bing Bong appeared. The pair came up with an idea – they could use Bing Bong's rocket wagon to fly out of the Memory Dump!

They sang loudly to power the rocket, but each time they flew up they couldn't quite reach the edge of the cliff.

They gave it one last try and, without Joy noticing, Bing Bong jumped out of the rocket wagon so it could reach the cliff.

As Joy looked back she saw Bing Bong in the dump far below.

"Go save Riley!" he called. "Take her to the Moon for me, okay?"

Joy had to grab Sadness, who was floating on a cloud, and get back to Headquarters.

As Family Island crumbled away, Joy spotted an Imaginary Boyfriend and had an idea.

Joy used the Boyfriend Generator to make hundreds of boyfriends. Using them as a huge tower, she swung towards Sadness....

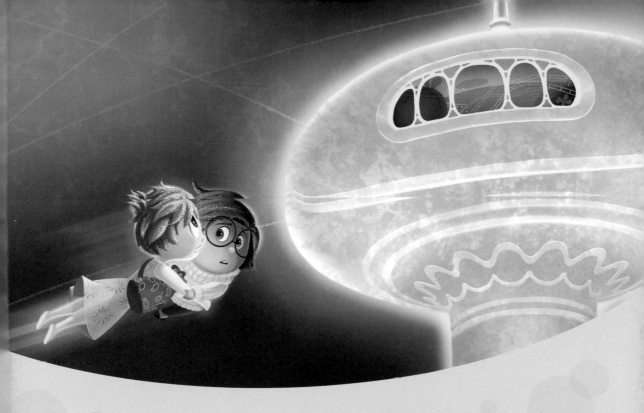

Joy grabbed hold of Sadness and the two of them flew through the air towards Headquarters. SPLAT! They hit the back window and started to slide down the glass.

Anger, Fear and Disgust ran towards the window. How were they going to get them inside?

Disgust had an idea! She got Anger really mad until flames burst out of him and used the fire to cut a hole in the window. Joy and Sadness climbed inside.

"Oh, thank goodness you're back!" cried Fear.

Joy looked up at the screen and saw that Riley was on the bus, ready to run away from home and back to Minnesota.

She realized that she had to let Sadness drive and let her step up to the console.

Sadness took a deep breath and pulled out the idea bulb. On the bus, Riley suddenly felt that she had to stay. "Wait!" she called to the driver. "I want to get off!"

As the other Emotions looked on, Joy handed the core memories to Sadness and they all turned blue. Sadness placed them back in the projector that played memories on the screen in Headquarters.

At Riley's house, Riley had just arrived back. Her mum and dad had been worried sick. She told them how she felt.

"I miss home," she said, remembering her life back in Minnesota.

Riley, Mum and Dad hugged each other and, at Headquarters, a brand-new core memory was created, which created a new Family Island.

A few days later, the Islands of Personality had reappeared – with a few new ones, too!

Joy, Sadness, Anger, Fear and Disgust were excited about the future. After all, Riley was 12 now ... what could happen?

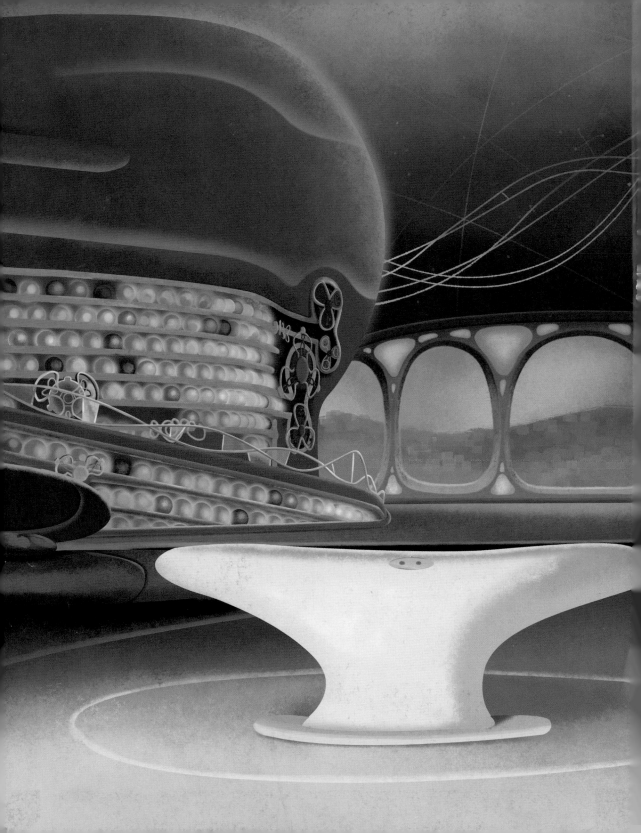